Still Just Grace

Still Just Grace

Written and illustrated
by
Charise Mericle Harper

Houghton Mifflin Company

Boston 2007

The text of this book is set in Dante.
The illustrations are pen and ink drawings digitally colored in Photoshop.

Library of Congress Cataloging-in-Publication Data
Harper, Charise Mericle.
Still just Grace / written and illustrated by Charise Mericle Harper.
p. cm.
Summary: When a struggling student teacher assigns a group project, third-
grader Just Grace gets so involved in working with Grace W. and Grace F. that
she fails to understand why she and her best friend, Mimi, are drifting apart.
ISBN-13: 978-0-618-64643-2 (hardcover)
ISBN-10: 0-618-64643-4 (hardcover)
[1. Best friends—Fiction. 2. Friendship—Fiction. 3. Teachers—Fiction. 4.
Schools—Fiction.] I. Title.
PZ7.H231323Sti 2007
[Fic]—dc22
2007012746

Manufactured in the United States of America
MP 10 9 8 7 6 5 4 3 2 1

For Ivy,
My empathy girl

ME

My real name is Grace, and if that was your real name then you would think that if someone wanted your attention they would shout "Grace!" but that is not what happens for me. I am not a usual person, but you can't tell that by just looking at me, because most of my unusualness is pretty much on the inside. My outside wrapping looks like any other girl's, except I don't wear very much pink because that is definitely not one of my favorite colors.

THINGS THAT ARE UNUSUAL
(SOME GOOD, SOME BAD, SOME NOT SURE)

1 Having four girls named Grace in the same class, and not letting any of them use the name Grace. Instead, calling them Grace W., Gracie, Grace F. (secretly named the Big Meanie by me, because that is what she is), and Just Grace. The Just Grace name probably being the most dumb name in the whole world ever, which is especially bad and sad because that's the one that is mine.

FOUR GRACES IN A ROW

ME

GRACE F.
BIG MEANIE

GRACIE

GRACE W.

2 Thinking that someone is 100 percent disgusting and not likable, and then having something happen that changes your mind a little bit so that the gross disgusting feeling is almost all gone, even when you have to stand right next to him and say, "Hi, Sammy."

3 Having a little superpower that almost no one knows about. Empathy power is the power to feel someone else's sadness, and then to try to make that sadness go away. It's not an easy power to have. I know, because I have it.

**USING MY EMPATHY POWER LAST WEEK
WHEN MOM MESSED UP DAD'S
BIRTHDAY CAKE**

MOM, DON'T WORRY. DAD WILL LIKE IT, EVEN IF IT'S DROOPY.

It still tasted good, though!

4 Girls who draw comics, because mostly that's a boy thing, though it just doesn't make any sense why it would be that way.

ONE OF MY NEW COMIC DRAWINGS

Butterfly Lady can make you feel better just by wrapping you in her big beautiful wings.

5 Living next door to your most perfect friend in the whole world. And having that friend be someone as great as Mimi.

ME AND MIMI

6 Having a cool French flight attendant named Augustine Dupre living right in your very own basement. But living in a great apartment that your dad made, not in the scary-spider part next to the furnace.

SPIDER

AUGUSTINE DUPRE

Hopefully they will never meet!

MYSTERY BOY
(SOUNDS BETTER THAN IT IS)

Mimi and I were watching the new people move into the house that the workers built right next door to her, where before there were just a bunch a weeds, broken glass, and prickle bushes.

NEW HOUSE   MIMI'S HOUSE   MY HOUSE

Actually, we were spying on them from her upstairs window, so they couldn't see us and we wouldn't have to talk to them.

Especially the mystery new boy who was going to be in our class. Mimi's mom was all excited about having new neighbors. She told Mimi she had to be nice to the new boy and let him play with us because he was going to be nervous and lonely. This did not sound like the kind of boy we wanted to play with. In my head I made a list of what could happen if you played with nervous, lonely creatures. It was not good.

LION

EAT YOU

BIRD

PECK YOU

DOG

BITE YOU

We saw the mom, the dad, and eight or nine moving people, but there was no boy. The moving people were like big ants and hard to count because they were all wearing the same blue shirt and not keeping still. "Maybe they left him at their old house," said Mimi. "Because he is terrible and they wanted to get rid of him," I said. "Because he is very gassy and has horrible breath," added Mimi. "And he burps and picks his nose!" I finished. "I'm glad he's not coming!" I said. "Me too!" said Mimi, and this made me secretly happy, because I did not want the new boy neighbor to be someone Mimi was going to like more than she liked me, her old girl neighbor.

MAGIC BOY
(STILL SOUNDS BETTER THAN IT IS)

Poof! Like magic, the next time we looked out the window we saw the boy. He was smiling and walking around the front lawn on his hands. He did not look nervous. The lonely part was hard to tell because that's an inside feeling so it's invisible. But most lonely people don't laugh and wave at strangers, which is what happened next, right after Mimi's mom pointed at the window where we were watching. Mimi's mom waved, the boy waved, and then they waited, looking at us, so we had to wave too. That's how the rule of waving works: you have to wave back if someone waves at you.

"He looks okay, like maybe he's fun,"

said Mimi. "I guess so," I said, but I looked out the window again just to make sure. "Oh, no! It's Sammy Stringer!" I cried. Sammy was talking to the new boy and Mimi's mom, and then Sammy was waving at us too. We waved, but then we made a pretend throw-up noise because you can't help but do that if something gets up there on your disgusto-meter.

MY DISGUSTO-METER CHART

HIGH

EATING A BUG ON PURPOSE.
EATING A BUG BY ACCIDENT.
STEPPING IN DOG POOP WITH BARE FEET.
SMELLING A SKUNK.
STEPPING IN DOG POOP.
SAMMY STRINGER.
MAYONNAISE ON A SANDWICH.

LOW

"We have to go down and say hello, or I'll get in trouble," said Mimi. "I know you hate Sammy Stringer, but you have to do this."

Then Mimi held my hand to give me some of her extra braveness. I used to hate Sammy Stringer. But now I just don't like him very much. It's not a big difference, and one day it might matter, but it didn't so much right then in that exact minute because I didn't want to talk to him, and, especially, I did not want him to call me Just Grace in front of the new boy.

SAMMY STRINGER SURPRISE

The first words out of Sammy Stringer's mouth were "Hey, Grace. Hey, Mimi. This is Max."

I couldn't believe that he didn't call me Just Grace, that he was being normal like a regular boy, and that his shirt wasn't covered in disgusting bits of food. This was all a big surprise for me. Mimi said hi. I said hi. Max said hi, and then Sammy said, "We're going to look at some stuff at Mrs. Luther's house."

Mrs. Luther is my neighbor on the side that is not next to Mimi's house. She is a teacher at our school, but she only teaches the kids that are older than us. Sammy likes her because she has collections of weird stuff like scary masks, animal poops, and other not regular stuff. And he probably also likes her because she makes amazing cookies that have real pieces of chocolate bars in them. I know about the cookies because I have tasted maybe ten of them, and they are excellent!

"Huh," said Mimi, and we watched them walk away. Sometimes when something completely unexpected happens your brain can't think of anything to say, so while your mouth is waiting for your brain it makes a little "huh" sound. So I knew what was happening in Mimi's head.

"Oh, well," I said. "That wasn't so bad." Sammy had been nice, Max had a new friend, and Mimi was still all mine. But maybe Mimi was thinking, *Now that fun handstand-walking Max boy won't be my new friend, and that disgusting and totally annoying Sammy Stringer is going to be hanging around next door.* I couldn't tell.

A PERFECT NIGHT

Mimi came over and we watched a new episode of *Unlikely Heroes,* which is our most favorite TV show ever. It's a show about real people who do things that usually only comic book heroes can do, and it's all 100 percent true.

This time there was a man who swam two whole miles in the ocean with a broken arm and a lady on his back. He had to save the lady when their boat tipped over because she couldn't swim and for some reason wasn't wearing a life jacket, which is a dumb thing to forget to wear if you don't know how to swim and you are on a boat in the middle of the ocean.

Then there was Sally, a pet parrot who pecked some robbers and kept them trapped in the house they were robbing until the police came to take them away. The owners of the parrot said Sally was a hero. Sally squawked, "Save me, Sweetie! Save me!" right on the TV, which is exactly what one of the robbers said when he was being attacked. The police said Sally was copying the robbers. Parrots love to copy sounds. Sally could also say, "Sally wants a biscuit" and "Hello, handsome," and make the beeping sound the microwave makes when the food is ready. Sweetie was the girl robber. They didn't say what the boy robber's name was. "Maybe Cupcake," joked Mimi.

WHAT IS GOING TO BE DIFFERENT AT SCHOOL

We are getting a student teacher for our class and his name is Mr. Frank. Mr. Frank is going to watch Miss Lois, our regular teacher, for a week, and then he is going to take over the whole class and teach it himself. Mr. Frank is a student teacher, which means he still goes to college, and still has to do homework, and is still mostly just learning about teaching stuff. This is good because it will be nice to have someone different and interesting for a change.

Miss Lois says student teachers have a lot of energy because they are young and fresh and full of new ideas. One of the new ideas I'm going to help Mr. Frank with is calling me Grace, or if I have to Grace S. for Grace Stewart. But I am definitely 100 percent not going to help him call me Just Grace!

WHAT WAS DIFFERENT AT SCHOOL

Mr. Frank was young and maybe fresh. I couldn't really tell that part, but the part I could tell right away was that Miss Lois was not going to let him use very many new ideas, especially when it came to changing names. As soon as I said, "Excuse me, Mr. Frank. I want to be called Grace or Grace S., please," Miss Lois said, "Now is not the time to be confusing everyone with new names." And then she said, "We will be keeping the same class name list even while Mr. Frank is here." Nobody seemed upset except me, but that is because I'm the only one with a stupid dumb name.

I looked over at Grace F. by mistake, and just like always, she was being mean. She was giving me a ha-ha smile right on her Big Meanie lips. Mr. Frank went around the room and introduced himself to everyone. I was not happy one bit when he said, "Hello, Just Grace. I'm happy to meet you," even though it's Miss Lois's rule and not his fault.

Once someone has started calling you one thing, it's almost impossible to get that person to change and call you anything different. So now of course I could tell that Mr. Frank was going to call me Just Grace forever and ever and ever. Even if I saw him on the street fifty-one years from now he was still going to say, "Excuse me, Just Grace, is that you?"

Then, to make everything even more worse, Mr. Frank kept calling Grace F. "Grace," instead of "Grace F." like he was supposed to. This was totally not fair to any of the other Graces, because Miss Lois said that no one could be called that. Grace F. seemed very happy that the mistake was happening and was all super chatty with Mr. Frank even though we didn't even know him yet. She was probably trying to put some kind of Big Meanie spell on him.

After lunch, Mr. Harris, the principal, brought Max to our class. He didn't get to sit next to Sammy because the only empty seat was the one next to the Big Meanie. I saw Sammy smile at Max, and then when none of the teachers was looking, Grace F. stuck her tongue out at Sammy. She probably thought he was smiling at her, which I know would never happen because even though Sammy

Stringer likes disgusting and unusual things, he would never in a billion years like anyone like the Big Meanie.

WHAT WAS DIFFERENT AT HOME

When I got home, I went right downstairs to visit Augustine Dupre. She is very good about making you feel better if something has happened that you do not like. She lets you talk and talk and talk until most of the unhappy feelings have been let out of your body in words.

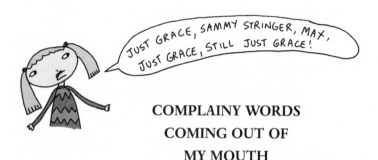

COMPLAINY WORDS
COMING OUT OF
MY MOUTH

Lots of people don't have time for this kind of thing, but Augustine Dupre is not a time rusher. When I finished telling her about how I was still probably going to be called Just Grace forever, she patted my arm and said, "Well, some time away will probably make you feel better." This is how I found out that I was going to miss three days of school and go on a trip to Chicago to visit my grandma.

WHY WE ARE GOING ON A VACATION AT A NOT NORMAL VACATION TIME

Mom says it is time for Grandma to move out of her house and into an apartment building, and that Grandma is going to be so much happier in a new, smaller apartment. She says there are lots of other old people living right in the same building, so Grandma won't be alone so much. She says they have movie nights, and dances, big dinners, and lots of art and music classes. It sounds a lot like summer camp except there are probably no bugs, and you don't have to go to a special building to use the bathroom.

I am thinking that maybe Grandma can make me a new wallet like the kind we made at camp last year, because my laces part got messed up and then the wallet couldn't open, which is not great because that is where the money is supposed to go. Plus, Grandma is good at sewing and making her fingers do exactly the right thing when they are holding string, or glue, or tiny little pieces of tape.

WALLET THAT GRANDMA COULD MAKE ME

MONEY GOES IN THIS SPACE

LITTLE COLORED LACES ALL AROUND THE EDGE. THIS IS THE PART I MESSED UP.

FLAP THAT FOLDS OVER TO SNAP THE WALLET SHUT

HEART ON THE BACK

OWL PICTURE ON THE FRONT

WHAT IS SUPER EXCELLENT

Telling everyone at school that you get to miss school and go on vacation is one of the best things ever. It's more special than going when it's regular vacation time, because you are the only one who gets to do it and everyone else has to stay and work on boring school stuff.

WHAT IS NOT SUPER EXCELLENT

Miss Lois gave me homework to do while I was gone. So now I have to take the boring school stuff with me, which is not as fun as I thought it was going to be. The only okay part of the homework is the project to write a two-page story about something smaller than a peanut butter sandwich.

This was one of Mr. Frank's new ideas, and it seemed like a good one, except a lot of kids weren't listening and got confused. They thought we were supposed to write a story about a peanut butter sandwich. Marta, the girl with the longest hair in our whole class, said, "Excuse me, Mr. Frank, but I'm allergic to peanuts, so I shouldn't write about them because I might get sick and then have to get a shot."

Miss Lois didn't even let Mr. Frank answer. She said, "Now, children, forget about the peanut butter sandwich and just write a story about something that is smaller than this square." And then she drew a square that was the same size as a peanut butter sandwich on the chalkboard.

SQUARE

SANDWICH

Mr. Frank looked unhappy and his face got red. Grace F. was looking at Mr. Frank at exactly the same time as I was. It looked like she gave him a secret smile to try to make him feel better, but it must have been a mistake, because there is no way the Big Meanie could have even one drop of empathy power inside her.

MIMI AND MAX

After school I told Mimi all about my big surprise vacation. I said, "I'm sorry I won't be here to watch *Unlikely Heroes* with you tomorrow night," but she didn't seem very sad about my being gone.

"Oh, that's okay," said Mimi. "Max is coming over with his parents for dinner, so I can watch it with him."

This was not what I was wanting to hear, so I said, "What if he doesn't like it? Lots of boys don't like that sort of show because the heroes don't wear costumes or capes or even have big muscles." Mimi surprised me 100 percent by what she said next. "Don't worry," she said. "He loves *Unlikely Heroes,* just like us. I already asked him. Isn't that great?" "Yeah," I answered, "great."

But I wasn't being even 50 percent truthful, because great is getting lots of amazing super-surprise presents when it is not even your birthday. Great is not having your next-door-neighbor-best-friend-in-the-whole world become best friends with her next-door-handstanding-boy-neighbor you have to go away on vacation.

SURPRISE PRESENTS

That night Mom said she had some surprise presents for me if I promised to be extra good on the drive to Chicago and not complainy when we drove by stuff that looked cool but didn't stop and get out of the car to see it. Stuff like a toothpick castle, a fairy land, a giant petrified forest, or even the world's largest sandwich. "Can I complain on the way back?" I asked. "No, it's a two-way deal," said Mom, and she held out a big sparkly bag with polka-dot tissue paper popping out the top. It's hard to say, "No deal," when you are looking at a bag filled with presents. So I said, "Okay, I promise."

The bag was filled with tons of great things, but the most excellent thing was the Supergirl underwear. It was exactly what I

SPARKLES

BAG OF CANDY

SUPER GIRL UNDERWEAR

PENS WITH LIGHT-UP TOPS

NICE DRAWING PAPER

NEW TOOTH BRUSH

HAIR BANDS

MYSTERY BOOK

SUPER GIRL JOURNAL

CAR BINGO GAME

had always wanted, and the same kind that the girl on *Unlikely Heroes* wore when she rescued a grown-up man from drowning! I called Mimi up on the phone to tell her right away, and then I held them up at my bedroom window so she could look out her bedroom window and see them.

That's when I remembered that my window and Mimi's window would always be across from each other, and this could never happen with Max's window unless Mimi's whole house was turned completely around, back to front. Turning a house around is not easy and would probably not happen, because Mimi's dad is very careful and full of worry about his lawn all the time. He would not be excited about a house project that would ruin his grass. And if you turned a whole huge house around, your lawn would be 100 percent turned into mud.

TURNING MIMI'S HOUSE AROUND

THE DRIVE TO CHICAGO

We drove for a while and then Mom told Dad we had to stop for dinner or she was going to faint with hunger. I had pizza and then pie and ice cream, but mostly ice cream, for dessert. When we got back in the car it was dark, which made it really hard to see anything interesting. It is hard not to think about stuff in your head when there is nothing else to do, like look out the window. I had two big thoughts:

1 Was this vacation really going to be fun?

2 Was something important going to happen back at home while I was gone?

These are not the most perfect kinds of things to be thinking right before you fall asleep, but it is what happened. When I woke up it was morning and we were driving right into the big city of Chicago.

The Welcome to Chicago sign would be even cooler if it had your name on it.

Grandma lives right near the middle of the city. If I were older, Dad said it would only take me fifteen minutes to ride my bike from Grandma's house right to the entrance of the tallest building in the whole United States. Mom would never in a million years let me ride my bike on the road, so I would have to do it in secret. The tallest building is called the Sears Tower, and from the top you can see everything in Chicago, because Chicago's ground is as flat as a pancake.

FLAT AS A
PANCAKE

HILLY LIKE
MASHED POTATOES

MOUNTAINOUS LIKE
AN ICE CREAM SUNDAE

PROMISE

Right before we got to Grandma's house Mom asked Dad to park the car on the side of the road so she could talk to me without worrying about if we were going in the right direction or not. She said three things:

1 "This move is going to be hard for Grandma, so please try to be cheerful."

2 "If Grandma gives you something to keep, just take it and say thank you, even if you don't want it. We can throw it away later."

3 "Don't say anything about Grandma's new apartment building, Shady Grove, unless the something you are going to say is a nice thing."

Then Mom said, "Do you promise?" and I said, "Yes, I promise."

Dad started up the car and we drove two more blocks until we got to Grandma's house. Then we drove around and around and around, and finally we had to park in the same spot where Mom had made the promise talk because there weren't any other places to park.

It's really hard to find a parking spot in Grandma's neighborhood because lots of people like to go to there. There are amazing stores and restaurants all over the place.

MAP OF WHERE THE AMAZING THINGS ARE
THAT I KNOW ABOUT

X Grandma's house.

1 Letizia's ice cream store/bakery (they have yummy everything!).

2 Store called Sparkly (everything in the whole store has sparkles on it). If you liked sparkles, then you would be crazy with joy the second you walked inside.

3 Lulu's Supply Shack — I am actually allowed to walk to this store by myself and buy stuff. They have normal things like cereal, milk, and candies.

4 Store that sells crazy lamps. It's fun to look in here even if you don't want to buy anything.

5 Comic book store — Grandma never lets me go in there because she said they only sell comics for grownups. It's on my list for when I'm grown up — I'm definitely going to go back there and go inside.

6 Coffee shop that has the best doughnuts in the whole world, even better than the doughnuts made in the doughnut store.

7 Art store. This is where I am sometimes allowed to buy art supplies when mine are all used up. If I were a famous artist I would for sure shop in here.

Two blocks is a long way to go if you have to carry lots of stuff, so it was good that we had the kind of suitcases with wheels. On the last block Mom raced me, but I won, so I got the first hug from the lady at the finish line. Of course it was Grandma.

MY FAVORITE THING ABOUT GRANDMA

Grandma always tells the truth, even if it could kind of hurt your feelings, which you might think is not good, but really it's okay, because she is not doing it to be mean. She just can't help it. She doesn't know how to tell a lie, even a teeny-tiny mini one. She says, "I've got truth serum in my veins—that's just how I was made."

It's kind of like my empathy power: sometimes it's a good power to have and sometimes it's not, but you can't pick and choose when you want it, because it's with you 100 percent of your whole life, which means always! And you have to live with it forever and let it be part of you, just like if you had big feet, stick-out ears, or long monkey arms. Except it is invisible, which is probably better, because people can't look at you and see it right away.

BIG FEET

STICK-OUT EARS

LONG MONKEY ARMS

THE SECOND THING GRANDMA SAID

The first thing Grandma said was "I'm so happy to see all of you." The second thing Grandma said was "I can't wait to move!" "Really?" asked Mom. "Really!" said Grandma, and I believed her because of the not lying power, but Mom, who has known Grandma her whole entire life, didn't seem sure. "Come on, I have a picnic in the backyard," said Grandma. "Race you," I yelled, but it really wasn't fair, because the first one through Grandma's side gate is always going to be the winner, and I was already there.

THINGS THAT ARE GOOD ABOUT PICNICS

Picnic food

Sitting outside

Cool air

Listening to the city

THINGS THAT ARE BAD ABOUT PICNICS

Ants

We had to move the picnic inside because Grandma's backyard is right on top of a giant underground ant farm. Grandma said they moved in last year and now the ant army is the biggest one she has ever seen. She said they probably can't wait until she leaves so that they can take over her house too! I especially don't like the big black ones. For some reason it's easier to squish a little ant than a big one. Grandma's ants were little, and she promised me that they did not go upstairs to where the bedrooms were. That was good news, because I did not want to worry about eating one when I was asleep. Not many people know this, but sleeping people eat bugs all the time. The bugs crawl into their mouth and then the sleeping people just swallow them up by accident. It's disgusting!

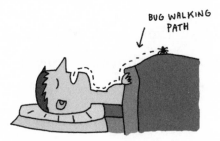

BUG WALKING PATH

Mostly this happens with little bugs.

WHAT WE DIDN'T KNOW ABOUT GRANDMA

Mom was surprised, Dad was surprised, and I was surprised. Grandma has a new friend who is a man, and he is a great packer! Almost everything in Grandma's whole house was in a box with a colored label on it and very nice printing on the label. Grandma doesn't like to pack, which is why Mom and

Dad brought their work gloves and lots of markers and tape, but now they didn't need any of that stuff. Grandma told Mom and Dad that they should go out for dinner and not to worry about us because she had a pizza ready to pop in the oven. She was getting rid of them so we could have some special time together, which I was happy about. I love having Grandma all for me. Mom loved the idea too, but first she said I had to do my schoolwork while she asked Grandma some questions.

These were Grandma's answers:

"Two months ago."

"At the grocery store near the canned tomatoes."

"Roger Costello."

"Nice-looking, nice smile."

"Shady Grove."

"Nine grandchildren."

"It's just him and Captain Furry."

From where I was sitting I could only hear Grandma's part of the talking, but it wasn't very hard to figure out what most of the questions were. The Captain Furry one was a mystery, though.

CAPTAIN HAT

CAPTAIN FURRY?

WHAT'S SO GREAT ABOUT TRENDY?

Mom said she and Dad were going to go somewhere fun and trendy. So I said, "What's so great about trendy?" Mom said that *trendy* was another word for popular, and that trendy restaurants were usually crowded with people who were famous, wished they were famous, or were hoping to see someone famous. She said there were at least ten trendy restaurants right near Grandma's house. After they left, Grandma said she didn't know anything about trendy but she knew what she liked, and what she was going to like after our pizza dinner was some tasty Italian ice cream. I said I was going to like that too!

WHAT WE TALKED ABOUT AT DINNER

I told Grandma all about still being called Just Grace, all about Mimi and Max, and all about Mr. Frank and the Big Meanie. It was a lot of stuff to tell, and it lasted from the first bite of pizza all through the walk to the bakery / ice cream store and right up until we were picking out our favorite flavors for dessert.

MY FAVORITES   GRANDMA'S FAVORITES

WHAT GRANDMA SAID

"The most important thing," said Grandma, "is to not be afraid of change. And sometimes change can be tricky. What looks like a bad change might really turn out to be a good change. It's always hard to tell at first— you have to let it sit for a while and see what happens." And then she said that being called Just Grace seemed a lot like a bad change and she was sorry about that. I was hoping she would tell me how to fix it, but she said she didn't know everything even though she had been around for a long time and was pretty old. I made a list in my head but I couldn't see how any of my bad changes were going to turn out to be good.

 Mr. Frank calling me Just Grace.

Mimi becoming best friends with Max.

The Big Meanie pretending to have empathy feelings and hating me at the same time.

SHE ALWAYS
HAS HER HAIR
DIFFERENT

WHAT WOULD HAVE BEEN GREAT

I know that this could never happen in real life, but I was hoping that Grandma would say, "I have just the thing to fix your problem," and then we'd go upstairs into her attic and she would give me a book with magic spells, a hypnotism ring, or some kind of special potion in a bottle, and then I would just follow some directions and everything could turn out exactly how I wanted.

WHAT GRANDMA GAVE ME

Some promises are harder to keep than other promises, but the promise to pretend to like what Grandma gave me was not even needed at all, because Grandma only gave me great stuff that I really for truly liked. Everything was in a box with my name scribbled in Grandma's messy handwriting on the side. I was glad that she made the box all by herself and didn't let her new packer man friend do it. My favorite thing in the whole box was Grandma's very own special silver heart locket on a chain. She said I could put a special picture in it and no one but me would know about it.

LOCKET GRANDMA GAVE ME

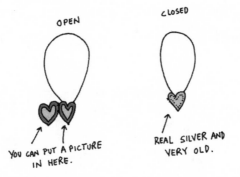

OPEN

CLOSED

YOU CAN PUT A PICTURE IN HERE.

REAL SILVER AND VERY OLD.

There was one special memory thing in the box. It was a poster I made for Grandma's dog Barnaby the time he ran after a squirrel and got lost by accident. We made sixty copies and put them everywhere we could think of until someone called and said he found him eating pizza out of a garbage can behind his house. Barnaby loved pizza crusts, which was good for me because that is the only part of the pizza I don't like. He died two years ago, and even though Grandma says she still misses him, she always smiles and laughs when we talk about him. She says it's because Barnaby made her days happy, which is exactly the perfect way for a pet to be.

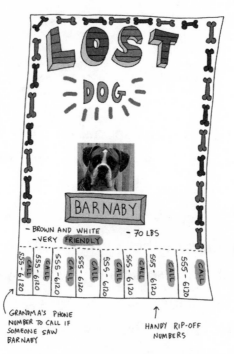

The other stuff in the box was two wooden treasure boxes, a red velvet pillow with a map of Arizona sewn on the front of it, Mom's vest with all her Girl Scout badges, five big balls of colored string, a not real leopard skin purse — real leopard skin would be gross for me because I love animals — a scrapbook album from Grandma's trip to New York when she was fifteen, lots of pens with little things inside them that moved, and a Supergirl T-shirt. The T-shirt was new and not an old thing because Grandma said they didn't have Supergirls when she was young.

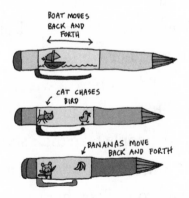

TRENDY RESTAURANT

Mom and Dad were very excited about their dinner. They saw one famous person, the man who used to do the weather on the TV news. Plus they said the food was spicy and very good, which means I would not have liked it one bit. Mom said the walls of the restaurant were painted red and the windows had big velvety curtains on them. It sounded a lot like Augustine Dupre's living room, which would be a very nice place to eat dinner if you were not worried about spilling something on her white carpet. Dad said the restaurant did not have a white carpet on the floor, which was probably a good idea if you don't make people take their shoes off before they eat. Augustine Dupre has a no-shoe rule if you want to walk on her carpet; this is how she makes it stay nice and clean.

SUPER ME

Today I was Supergirl from my insides, which no one could see, to my outsides. I wore my new Supergirl underwear and my new Supergirl T-shirt both at the same time. The moving people got to the house really early and started putting everything with a red label on it into the truck. Grandma's packer friend was super good at organizing. He even made a color chart that explained all about the labels.

 Green label means . . . donate it to someone needy, who might like it even if Grandma or no one in our family wants it anymore.

Red label means . . . Grandma is keeping it with her and taking it to her new Shady Grove apartment.

Yellow label means . . . it goes in the garbage.

Orange label means . . . Mom and Dad have to look at it and decide if they want to take it back home with us.

If they don't want it, they have to put on a new yellow label or a new green label.

While Mom and Dad looked at all the orange labels, I went upstairs to work on my story for school. For some reason all I could think about was ants, so it's a good thing that an ant is smaller than a peanut butter sandwich. Mr. Frank didn't say the whole story had to be just words, so I drew a comic,

because one of my most favorite parts about
making stories is the drawing pictures part.

58

ANOTHER EASY PROMISE

Grandma's new Shady Grove apartment was fantastic, and I said that right after we finished getting the tour. Mom and Dad were smiling too, because the only things anyone could ever say about Shady Grove were great and amazing things. It was nothing like camp. It was fancy! And not fancy like you were scared to touch anything, but more just fancy like you wanted to say, "Wow! This is fancy." And then maybe do a twirl if nobody was watching. We all had breakfast with

Grandma and her new packer friend, Mr. Costello, in a covered garden outside. Mr. Costello was very nice but very furry. He had white fur all over his sweater and pants and even a bit sticking out of one eyebrow. I wanted to ask about it but wasn't sure if it was a nice question to ask or a not nice question to ask, so I didn't say anything. Eating outside was like a picnic except there were no ants, which is something Grandma was very happy about for sure.

NO WALLET FOR ME

After lunch we went to look at the arts and crafts room, where Grandma will get to make some projects. I asked the craft teacher lady if Grandma was going to make a beaded bookmark or a wallet but she said they didn't make that kind of thing. Instead Grandma can make paintings, or bowls, or even necklaces with real jewels. The craft lady gave me a cord necklace with an Indian bead head on it. It looked a little bit like something my next-door neighbor Mrs. Luther might wear, but I still liked it. I was only a little bit disappointed about the wallet, but I didn't say anything because mostly I was pretty happy.

WHAT WE DID THE REST OF THE DAY

We went to the zoo, which was great because it was free and that meant Mom and Dad had extra money for me to spend. I picked out two presents in the gift shop, one for me and one to bring back for Mimi.

VERY VERY
COZY. NOT
LIKE A REAL
POLAR BEAR

HANDS OPEN
AND CLOSE
SO MONKEY
CAN HOLD ON
TO STUFF

**STUFFED POLAR
BEAR FOR ME**

**MONKEY WITH
PINCH PAWS FOR
MIMI**

After the zoo visit it was already lunchtime. Grandma wanted us to come back and have lunch with her and Mr. Costello, but Dad wanted to get a hot dog from his favorite Chicago hot dog restaurant. Mom said we should go back and eat at Shady Grove because this was a trip about Grandma and not a trip about eating hot dogs. This was easy for her to say because she doesn't like hot dogs very much anyway. Dad secret-whispered to me that we would get a hot dog before we left, PROMISE.

I asked Dad about Mr. Costello and why he was so furry but he said he hadn't noticed. I don't know how not, but sometimes grownups just don't see stuff. When I asked Dad if he knew anything about Captain Furry he said, "Is that one of the characters on that TV cartoon show that your mother doesn't like?" Obviously he didn't know anything at all. Maybe Captain Furry was a secret spy name for Mr. Costello? Maybe Captain Furry was a superhero who sprayed his enemies with fur, and Mr. Costello was an enemy? Maybe Captain Furry was something really amazing and cool?

INSIDES OUT

The new people who bought Grandma's house are going to take all the insides out of the house and throw them in the garbage, even the walls. Right after Grandma told me this she gave me a special photo book she made just for me. It was filled up with pictures of the inside of her house before everything was packed away. That way, Grandma said, I would never forget how it looked. Mom cried when she looked at the book, but it didn't seem sad to me. When Grandma saw Mom crying she started crying too, so I tried to do something cheerful to help them. I put Mimi's present on the end of my nose and pretended it wasn't there. I'm glad they looked and smiled right away, because the little monkey paws were pinching extra hard and making me have to breathe out of my mouth, which was not so easy, because it was filled up with turkey sandwich. After lunch Grandma took me to meet the mysterious Captain Furry.

CAPTAIN FURRY

Captain Furry is not a spy, not a superhero, and not something really amazing and cool. Captain Furry is a cat. A cat with crazy long hair who lives in the same apartment with Mr. Costello. I am glad I am not allergic to cats, because just looking at Captain Furry could make cat-allergic people sneeze and their eyes puff up like grapefruits — which are fruits I do not like, even with lots of sugar on them. Mr. Costello's living room is full of Captain Furry fur. Mr. Costello is full of Captain Furry fur. Even I was full of Captain Furry fur after only petting Captain Furry for just twenty seconds. You have to really be in love with a cat to live with that much fur in your world.

Captain Furry's best trick is that he jumps from the floor right up into Mr.

Costello's arms. Mr. Costello said that Captain Furry has lots of other tricks, like hiding in grocery bags and sleeping on pillows, but really those are just normal cat things and not tricks at all. But I didn't say that because I was trying to be polite.

NOT A TRICK

PAPER BAG

On our last night in Chicago we all went to a carnival: me, Grandma, Mom, Dad, Mr. Costello, and lots of Captain Furry's fur. The real Captain Furry had to stay home because cats can't go to carnivals. We found out about the carnival because there was a big poster for it right on the bulletin board near

Grandma's new arts and crafts room. Posters are a great way to get people's attention about stuff, because they are hard to miss seeing.

Mr. Costello says he brushes Captain Furry every week but still each time he gets enough fur on the brush to make a whole new mini Captain Furry.

CAPTAIN FURRY   BRUSH   MINI CAPTAIN FURRY

Dad and I went on most of the rides. Mom says she just likes to watch, which makes no sense, because I watched some of the big kids on the big rides and that was like having no fun at all. When I get taller there are two rides I am definitely going to go on for sure. One is called the Zipper and the other is called the Gravo-Force. On the Zipper you get to sit in a cage and spin all over like crazy; upside down, sideways, backwards, everything. On the Gravo-Force you stand up against the wall and get spun around really fast like you are in a washing machine and then suddenly the floor drops away from your feet. But the amazing thing is you don't fall down. You just stay there stuck up on the wall. And then when the ride slows down you just slide down the wall until your feet touch the floor again.

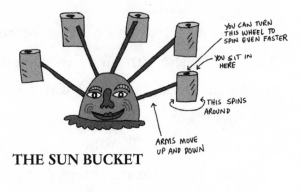

YOU CAN TURN THIS WHEEL TO SPIN EVEN FASTER

YOU SIT IN HERE

THIS SPINS AROUND

ARMS MOVE UP AND DOWN

THE SUN BUCKET

My favorite ride that I went on.

I had so much fun I could hardly stand it! It would have been better if Mimi were there, but Dad was good about being my partner, and he didn't start feeling sick until the very last ride, which was the octopus and not even scary. Mom said we could have any kind of junk food we wanted for dinner. I had a hot dog, but Dad said it wasn't going to be the same as a hot dog from his favorite place. Dad didn't eat anything because he was feeling green, which means he was feeling like he might throw up.

Grandma and Mr. Costello didn't go on any rides, not even the Ferris wheel, which you can go on even if you are a tiny baby. Mr. Costello likes to organize and write labels, but he does not like high places. Grandma said she didn't mind staying on the ground with him even after Mom and I said she could ride with us. Grandma was being a good friend, because I know for sure that she likes being on the very top of the Ferris wheel a whole lot more than being on the boring ground.

It was one of the best vacation days ever in my whole life. At night we all slept in Grandma's new apartment, except for Mr. Costello and Captain Furry. They slept in their own apartment two floors higher up than us. Grandma said that Mr. Costello was not afraid of his apartment even though it was even higher up than hers. Grandma said it was because it was not tippy and swingy like the Ferris wheel and so that made it okay for him.

NOT A NORMAL BREAKFAST

For the whole trip I kept all the promises I made to Mom, which was not at all hard to do, and then right before we started driving home Dad kept his promise to me. We went to his favorite hot dog restaurant and had hot dogs for breakfast. We were the only ones there, because eight o'clock in the morning is not a usual time to eat a hot dog. It was strange but they still tasted pretty good. I only put ketchup on mine.

WHAT YOU ARE SUPPOSED TO PUT ON A CHICAGO HOT DOG

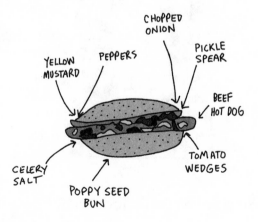

CHOPPED ONION

PICKLE SPEAR

PEPPERS

YELLOW MUSTARD

BEEF HOT DOG

CELERY SALT

POPPY SEED BUN

TOMATO WEDGES

THE DRIVE BACK HOME

I had hardly even thought about them when we were with Grandma, but as soon as we started driving back home all my problem worries rushed back into my head. I started thinking about Mimi and that handstanding Max. Maybe he was teaching her how to do it and now they were going to be handstanding new best friends.

MIMI WEARING HER FAVORITE PANTS

I started thinking about still being called Just Grace, and I started thinking about Mr.

Frank and the Big Meanie and her pretend empathy feelings. All the thinking made me wish that Dad would drive faster so we could get home sooner and I could find out if everything was just the same as when we'd left. I

MY BAD DRAWING

tried to draw, because that usually makes me feel better, but the car was too bumpy and I kept drawing squiggly lines by mistake. So instead I just had to play with Mimi's present.

Then I must have been asleep because Mom woke me up and said it was time to have some lunch. Grandma made us some sandwiches, but she forgot and put mayonnaise on mine, so I could only eat around the edges of it because mayonnaise is a food that is disgusting.

After lunch Mom and I played license plate bingo. I won all three games because she kept forgetting about playing and wasn't paying attention to the cars. Doing nothing sitting in a car makes you hungry a lot, so we stopped for dinner when it was only four-thirty, which is normally a time for snacks and not normally a time for a whole dinner. Dad said driving across the country is pretty boring. I think being the passenger when you are driving across the country is even more boring.

WHAT I SAW WHEN I GOT HOME

Nothing. It was dark out and three in the-morning and Mimi's house looked exactly the same as always. It was not turned around, which I was happy about.

WHAT I WANTED TO SEE ON MY VERY OWN FRONT DOOR

GRACE I MISSED YOU! YOU ARE MY BEST FRIEND FOREVER ♥MIMI

WHAT I SAW IN THE MORNING

Sammy Stringer, Max, and Mimi all talking together on Mimi's front steps. Mimi looked surprised to see me, like maybe she forgot I was coming home, or maybe she didn't see our car parked in front of our house, which is pretty hard to miss because it is red and not silver or tan or black like most cars.

But then Mimi screamed my name and came running over, and it seemed like everything was going to be okay and normal. But I was 100 percent wrong! Max and Sammy followed Mimi's footsteps all the way across the yard until they were standing right next to us, which was not what I was expecting.

When Mimi and I went inside to get

MIMI CHOO-CHOO

Mimi's present, Max and Sammy followed us through the front door, up the stairs, and right into my very own private all-girl bedroom. And the most surprising thing ever was that Mimi didn't even seem to notice. The only good part about it was that Mimi liked her present. Usually Mimi and I just stay in my room forever, but I did not want Sammy Stringer to sit on my bed or to even look at any of my special-to-me things, so I took Mimi back downstairs and into the kitchen before he could touch anything.

When Max saw the fridge, he said he was thirsty and asked for a drink. Of course I know how to be a good hostess so I gave everyone a big cup of orange juice with ice. Mimi asked me lots of questions about my vacation, but it wasn't as fun to talk about it when Sammy and Max were right there listening. Sammy saw my new bead-head necklace and said, "Hey, what's that? Is it from Mrs. Luther?"

I know it's not good to lie, but I couldn't help it, and plus this was a special bad occasion so I said, "No! It's a magic necklace. My

 grandma gave it to me." And then I said, "If I hold the bead head in my hands, close my eyes, and make a wish, then my wish will come true. Watch."

And then I closed my eyes and made a pretend wish that he would leave.

"What'd ya wish for?" asked Max. "Yeah, I don't see anything different," said Sammy. "It's like birthday wishes," I said. "You have to keep the wish a secret!" It was unbelievable how they could not see even one little bit how annoying they were being to me. "Well, I believe you," said Mimi, and then she said, "Do you want to come over after lunch and watch *Unlikely Heroes*?" "Sure," I said, and that made me feel happy again. But then both Max and Sammy said "Sure" too, and I was not feeling so happy again after all. "Great!" said Mimi. "See you later." And then they walked out the door all together. And Sammy was gone just like I wished he would be, except that Max and Mimi were gone too. The Mimi-being-gone part was not what I wanted at all.

WISH NECKLACE

When something happens that is strange or unusual but not magic it is called a coincidence. A coincidence is having no money and really wanting ice cream, and then finding fifty cents on the sidewalk, which is the perfect amount to buy a soft cone from the ice cream truck, which just happens to drive by in the next minute. Actually, that would really be two coincidences put together, which would be even more unusual and amazing.

1 Finding the fifty cents on the sidewalk.

2 The truck driving by right then.

These kinds of things do not happen very often, so when they do, most people who are good at paying attention, notice them. Wishing on the bead head and having the wish maybe come true was probably a coincidence, but I made another wish to test it out, just in case it really was filled with magical power. I closed my eyes and, holding the bead head the exact same as before, I wished for a swimming pool right in my very own backyard. This would be an excellent wish to come true, since swimming is one of my five most favorite things to do for exercise. I hardly ever get to swim because the only swimming pool I can go to is three miles away from my house and that is way too far for me to ride on my bike. That's what Mom says, and she gets to be the boss of me about stuff like that until I'm all grown up.

When I opened my eyes the yard was still filled with only grass and weeds, just like always. No swimming for me. But I kept the bead-head necklace on, because even pretend magic could maybe be better than no magic at all.

HELP WANTED

What I really, really needed was to be wearing my Supergirl underwear so I could have an amazing idea about how to make Sammy and Max disappear from Mimi, but Mom hadn't finished the laundry yet from our vacation, so I couldn't. And even though I thought about it real hard, all the time through lunch, my brain couldn't think up anything good. I tried to draw a comic to make myself feel better, but that didn't work either.

After lunch I walked over to Mimi's house because being with Mimi, Max, and Sammy was still better than being all alone without Mimi. Plus I didn't want to miss *Unlikely Heroes*. Maybe if Max and Sammy didn't talk while we were watching I could pretend they weren't even there.

WHAT MIMI SAID

Max and Sammy left after we watched three whole episodes of *Unlikely Heroes*. Mimi and I had seen them all before, but that's okay because they were still good. They were new for Max and Sammy, which made them not true *Unlikely Heroes* fans, because if you watched the show every week you would for sure have seen those episodes already.

I was secretly wondering about Max being an *Unlikely Heroes* fan when Mimi said, "Can you believe Max only ever saw *Unlikely Heroes* one time before he moved here?" It was probably another one of those coincidences, but I was holding the bead head right when she answered my thought question.

I wanted to ask Mimi why Max and Sammy were following her around so much, but this was not an easy question to ask. I touched the bead head, hoping that it would make her give me the right answer again. She said, "That Sammy Stringer really isn't so bad once you get to know him. I don't even think he picks his nose anymore, because I would notice something like that and I haven't seen him do it." This was not the right answer.

Then she said, "Max is teaching us and we can almost do walking handstands like him." This was not the right answer either, and especially not something I wanted to hear, because I can't even do a standing-still handstand, or a cartwheel, or anything where the arms of the body are supposed to hold up the whole rest of the body.

Mimi asked me to stay for dinner, but then I couldn't and had to go home because her eyes puffed up and she started sneezing over and over again. It looked like she was allergic to me, but her mom pointed at my shirt and said it was probably just the cat fur.

WISH

When I went home I had one big wish, but the necklace was for sure not going to be able to help.

I wished I hadn't gone away on vacation, but then at the last minute I changed it because then I wouldn't have seen Grandma in her new apartment. And when I'm talking to her on the phone or thinking about her I like to be able to know exactly where she is. It makes her seem not so far away.

After dinner I tried to do a handstand, but that didn't work out like it was supposed to either.

MR. FRANK'S NEW IDEA

While I was away on vacation I missed a lot of Mr. Frank's new ideas. He had even more new ideas today, but none of them had anything to do with not calling me Just Grace, because as soon as I walked into the classroom he said, "Welcome back, Just Grace."

The new idea that I didn't miss, and I wish I did miss, was that the whole class had to pair up with partners and come up with a project that had something to do with language. This sounded like it could maybe be a project about talking, but if you thought that you would be wrong. Mr. Frank's language project had to be about words, letters, or communication (which is a word that means how information goes from one person to another person). You weren't allowed to just stand in front of the class and talk about stuff or sing the alphabet song — those kind of things didn't count. Mr. Frank said we had to use words that were written down. Plus he said he wanted to see some creativity. Not everyone was happy, especially Abigail Whitkin, because right away she started to whine about not being able to sing the alphabet song for her project. She is one of those people who knows how to sing the whole thing backwards, which is not amazing but still kind of cool. So it would have been easy for her to show off her talent in front of the whole class and not do any extra work.

But the most terrible part of all was that while I was gone on my vacation, everyone had already picked their project partners. Mr. Frank asked everyone to stand in their groups, and that's when I saw Mimi and Max and Sammy all standing together. Mr. Frank said I had to join a group that had only two people in it. There was only one two-person group in the whole class, and it was the one group I would have never picked even in a million years. Having your teacher stand right next to you can make your feet do things they wouldn't normally want to do, so my feet walked across the room and stood next to Grace W. and the Big Meanie. It made my insides feel unhappy from head to toe!

Big Meanie Bossy-Pants

The Big Meanie was horrible and wanted to do all of the deciding about what the project was going to be all by herself. Mr. Frank said we had to pool our talents and our interests, which means we had to find a project that we all liked and could do all together, but the Big Meanie was not listening. Her big idea was that we should make a hair salon and give everyone in the class fancy hairstyles. This was a dumb idea and one that was not pooling our talents because Grace W. and I don't know anything about fancy hair and always wear our hair in exactly the same way every single day. Plus boys don't like anyone to mess with their hair and make them look all pretty. The Big Meanie said we could make up one hairstyle for each letter in the alphabet. Then she gave us both a piece of paper with drawings of girls' heads with different hairstyles on it. She said, "Just Grace, Grace W., pay attention!"

I didn't want to say it but the first thing

I thought about when I saw the paper was *Wow! The Big Meanie is even better at drawing than I am.*

Then she said, "You two have to practice some of these hairstyles tonight. And I'll think of the creative alphabet names." She was being 100 percent bossy, so I said, "You are not the boss of me!" Both Mr. Frank and Miss Lois looked over because I think I said it kind of loud, and we would have for sure gotten in trouble if the Big Meanie hadn't made a pretend smile and put her arm over my shoulder like we were best friends, which for sure we were not! "Quick, look happy," said the Big Meanie, and both Grace W. and I made pretend smiles. She was being bossy again but this time it seemed like maybe it was for a reason, so we let her. Just to see what was going to happen next.

REAL SMILE   **PRETEND SMILE**

If you know someone really well you can tell the difference.

MR. FRANK

The Big Meanie told us all about Mr. Frank and how she didn't want him to get into any more trouble with his new ideas not working out. She said that Mr. Frank had tried lots of new ideas but that Miss Lois wasn't looking like she liked most of them, and when Miss Lois didn't like an idea she took the class back from Mr. Frank and that made his face get all red and sad.

In two weeks Miss Lois was going to give Mr. Frank a grade just like she gave us, and if she gave him something bad like an F or a D then he would never get to be a teacher and would probably have to go work at the grocery store at night, putting boxes and cans on the shelves.

GOOD GRADES	OKAY GRADES	BAD GRADES

The Big Meanie said this was why we had to pretend to be liking each other and liking the project. I was very surprised, but she was right: this was a very good reason. I looked at Mr. Frank and I could tell he looked unhappy, or maybe he was just mad at Abigail Whitkin because she had started humming the alphabet song. If someone is humming the alphabet song, your brain just wants to sing along and you can't make it stop, no matter how hard you try. It's annoying! Right then I felt sorry for him and my empathy power just started right up. "We have to help him," I said, and then I let both of the Graces tell me about some of Mr. Frank's not-working-out new ideas that I had missed when I was away on my vacation.

MR. FRANK'S NEW IDEAS THAT MISS LOIS DIDN'T LIKE

1 Saying that anything with words on it can be used in reading class. Miss Lois says magazines and comic books do not count

for reading, and she was very not happy when John Traffie brought in three cereal boxes with puzzles on the back for his reading project.

2 Having everyone in the class make up a new crazy name for themselves with this formula that was supposed to help us learn about the different parts of a sentence:

An adjective (which is a describing word) + a participle (which is an action word and kind of a verb) + the first letter of your name added to "umble" if it's a consonant or the first letter of your name added to "cky" if it's a vowel + a noun (which is a thing) + the name of some kind of pastry.

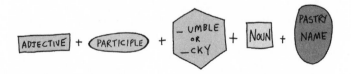

Miss Lois especially didn't like Brian Aber's made-up name, which was

Slimy Oozing Bumble Butt Cake.

My name would have been something much more creative and beautiful, but after a couple of the boys used endings like Booger Pie and Poop Cookie Miss Lois said the name project was over, so I didn't get a chance to make up a name. Poop Cookie sounded a lot like something Sammy Stringer's brain would think up.

WHAT GIRLS THINK UP	WHAT BOYS THINK UP

3 Asking the class to draw something from their imagination that they wished was real. Kids drew superheroes, and fairies, and friendly monsters and stuff like that, but when Isabella drew a unicorn Sandra Orr said, "You can't draw a unicorn! Unicorns are real! You have to pick a made-up thing!" Mr. Frank came over and told Sandra that he was pretty sure that unicorns were not real, but then Sandra started to cry and said that her mom had seen one so he was wrong, they were real!

Sandra was crying so hard, Miss Lois had to take her out of the classroom and walk her to the nurse's office. When Miss Lois came back she said everyone should put the imagination creatures away and just draw a favorite zoo animal instead. Grace W. said Mr. Frank's face was very red.

Nobody said any-
thing more about uni-
corns for the whole
rest of the day, and
when Sandra came to
school today she was

wearing a white sweatshirt with a unicorn
and a rainbow on it.

THREE GRACES

I was pretty sure that it wouldn't work, but I
held on to the bead head just like before and
wished that Mr. Frank would be okay. I
wished that his face would not get red
because of this new idea, and I wished that
he would not have to get a job putting cans
and boxes on the grocery store shelves at

night. I made all my wishes for Mr. Frank because he seemed to need wishes more than I did, and now I was filled with empathy power for him.

The Big Meanie saw me closing my eyes and said, "Grace, what are you doing?" I was 100 percent surprised that she called me Grace and not Just Grace like she normally did. It was like she forgot that she was the Big Meanie and filled with hate for me.

I said, "I'm just trying to think of how to help Mr. Frank and come up with an idea for our project that uses all of our pooling of talents. Grace and I don't know anything about hairstyles." I thought she might be mad, but she just looked at both of us and then said, "Grace, I see what you mean." And for some reason, that just made us start calling each other Grace as much as we could. It was confusing but very fun. "So, Grace, what do you think we should do?" "I don't know, Grace. How about something big?" "Grace, do you think Grace means a big sign or some kind of huge poster?" "Yes, Grace, I think Grace does. Let's do something that will get everyone's attention, okay, Grace?"

All this Grace talking made me sad that we couldn't use our normal Grace names like this all the time, and I said, "I sure wish I wasn't called Just Grace. It's unfair that I lost my real name!" "Mine too!" said Grace. "And mine three," said Grace. And then right there, because of everything we had just said, I had the start of an idea.

THE PROJECT IDEA

Grace and Grace loved the idea. And we made a promise to keep it a three Grace secret until we were ready to show everybody what it was.

SURPRISE

Mimi said she was sorry that I couldn't be in her group with Max and Sammy. Then she said she was sorry that I had to be in a group with the Big Meanie and I said, "Grace F. isn't really a big meanie all the time." "I'm surprised," said Mimi, and I could tell that she really was.

MIMI'S PROJECT

Mimi said that she and Max and Sammy were doing a human alphabet for their project. She said that she was trying to keep it a secret to surprise me, but that now that she could almost do a handstand she couldn't make herself not tell me. She said that handstanding was important because they were going to make their bodies be all the letters of the alphabet, from A to Z and then shout out all the adjectives they could think of that started with that letter. Mimi said that some of the letters were harder than others and right now they had practiced all the way to *K*, which was kind of a hard one. She said the letters were pretty easy to do if you did them lying down on the ground but a lot harder when you did them standing up, which is what they were going to do. She said it was lucky that Max was so good at handstanding because that helped a lot.

HOW THREE BODIES COULD MAKE A *K*

← NOT SO EASY

Right when Mimi was about to ask me what my project was going to be she started sneezing. She pointed to my shirt and I could see that it had Captain Furry fur on it. How or why is a mystery, because it was a clean shirt that hadn't even gone on the trip with me to Chicago. In between sneezes Mimi said that I could come to her house after school and watch her, Max, and Sammy practice the *L* and *M* and *N* part of the alphabet. "I'll try," I said, and suddenly it didn't even make me super sad that Mimi was going to be with Max and Sammy again. Because now I knew the real reason they were being together all the time. You can't be a human alphabet without practice. Mimi was just busy with her project, just like I was going to be busy with the other Graces.

WHAT WAS LUCKY

It was lucky that Mimi started sneezing at the exact time she did, because I didn't want to have to say, "I can't tell you what my project is because it is a three Grace secret." Plus I didn't want to tell her why I was going to have to go to the grocery store after school and ask for nineteen empty boxes.

Nineteen boxes = one for everyone in the class, even Mr. Frank and Miss Lois.

IF YOU LEARN A LESSON YOU SHOULD TRY NOT TO FORGET IT

If you get in trouble with your parents for something, it is a good idea to try to remember what it was for so you don't make that exact same mistake again another time. Once I got into trouble for walking all over my neighborhood without permission, so now I know exactly what to do. This time I asked Mom first. Mom said she would walk with me to the grocery store, but then Augustine Dupre was standing outside and said she needed to go too. I guess Mom didn't really want to go, because when she heard this, she gave me some money and a list of two things to buy and a quick goodbye wave.

Augustine Dupre said, "You must be buying a lot of groceries if you need to bring that wagon. How many things are on your list?" "Two," I said. "Just strawberry jelly and mustard. The wagon is for the empty boxes. I need nineteen of them." And then I told Augustine Dupre all about the project. It was breaking the Grace secret, but Augustine Dupre was not going to tell anybody one word about it because she is the number one best secret keeper I have ever met. She said, "What an interesting idea." And that made me happy because I thought so too.

When we got home it was almost dinnertime and too late to go over to Mimi's house. I didn't see her or even hear anyone in her yard, so they were probably already all finished with the alphabet practice.

FANCY HANDWRITING

After dinner I took all the boxes into Augustine Dupre's apartment. Augustine Dupre can do perfect fancy handwriting just like Grandma's new friend Mr. Costello, so I asked her to write the numbers on the front of the boxes for me.

MY   **AUGUSTINE DUPRE'S**

NUMBER 13   **NUMBER 13**

When we were finished Augustine Dupre helped me put all the boxes in Mom's car so Mom could drive me to school with them tomorrow. Augustine Dupre is always helpful and thoughtful and filled with energy, just like Mr. Frank and even Grandma. Even though Grandma is kind of old and doesn't have much running-around energy, she is filled with lots of helpful energy. Plus, she is smart, because right now some of my bad changes looked like they were maybe turning into good changes, just like she said they could. And the most surprising one was about the Big Meanie, who had stopped being a Big Meanie right in front of my very own eyes. When I told her, Grandma wasn't going to hardly believe it!

WHAT I FORGOT

The next day I was so excited about bringing my boxes to school that I forgot to check my clothes to make sure they did not have any Captain Furry fur on them. I remembered about that part after I was talking to Mimi and she started sneezing. She wanted to tell me all about being a human *W* but I had to move away from her and then Miss Lois got mad and said, "No shouting in the hallway." If there are yes-people and no-people, Miss Lois is for sure in the no-person group. Mr. Frank is a yes-person.

Grace who used to be the Big Meanie said that Mr. Frank is her most favorite teacher ever and that she knows a secret about him but she is not allowed to tell it to anyone at school. I asked if she could tell us the secret if she was not at school and maybe at my house instead. When she said, "I think so," I invited both the Graces to my house after school.

WHAT IS IMPOSSIBLE

It is impossible to pick every piece of Captain Furry fur off your shirt. As soon as you let  it go with your fingers it flies right back and lands somewhere else on your shirt.

Because of this happening I couldn't sit next to Mimi at lunch. It is impossible for a person to chew and swallow a sandwich while she is sneezing so I sat in the middle of Grace and Grace instead. I forgot that I was wearing my bead-head necklace until I saw Mimi sitting all alone at her table. As soon as I saw her sadness I closed my eyes and wished for Max and Sammy to sit with her, which was a wish I would have never thought that I would make. Not ever. Then like magic I saw Sammy and Max walk over to Mimi with their lunch bags. Mimi saw me looking at her and waved with a big smile on her face like maybe she knew about my wish. But she couldn't have, because Mimi is not a mind reader and I know that for sure. And even though my wishes were happening all around me like crazy, it was probably just another one of those coincidences.

Right then the Grace who used to be the Big Meanie asked if she could wear my bead-head necklace for a while. I was going to say, "No, my grandma gave it so me," but then I remembered about that part not being true. Grandma hadn't given me the bead-head necklace; she'd given me her special silver locket, which I had 100 percent forgotten all about. The bead head was from the craft lady, so it really wasn't special except for maybe being magic, which it probably wasn't anyway. It took a long time to think about all this stuff, which for sure made Grace think I was trying to think up a nice way to say no. She seemed really surprised when I said yes and took it off to give it to her.

THE PROJECT AT SCHOOL

In the afternoon Mr. Frank reminded everyone that the next day was going to be the start of the project presentations. We all already knew this because he had said the same thing right before we all went to the lunchroom for lunch. He seemed nervous that the class was going to mess up another one of his new ideas, but he didn't have to worry about us.

We three Graces were ready for our project. I had the boxes with the numbers already done and sitting in the cloakroom, and the other Graces had finished their parts of the project too. Grace had written each number (1 to 19) on a little card and Grace had made the special posters at the copy store. We decided that Grace should make the posters because she was so good at drawing, and even though we didn't use her idea for the hair salon, we still thought that the hairstyles drawings she made were pretty excellent.

At the end of class Mr. Frank came over and asked us how we were doing with our project. By mistake he called Grace "Grace" again and not Grace F. like he was supposed to, but this time it didn't make me grumpy like before.

SOMETHING NEW AT MY HOUSE

I had never before in my life had anyone else with the name of Grace in my house, and then today there were three of us. I introduced each new Grace to Mom and she said, "Oh my, this is a little bit confusing. How does this work at school?" But before either of the other Graces could answer I said we had to go upstairs to work on some home-work.

I didn't want Mom to know that my name at school was Just Grace. It was exactly the kind of thing that would make her mad, and then she would go to the school and complain. And even though I 100 percent don't like the name Just Grace, having Mom come to the school all angry about it would be worse. Only babies complained about stuff like that to their mom, and I was not a complainer baby!

MY ROOM

I let the other Graces sit on my bed and even touch my things, and it did not bother me one little bit. Grace had the bead-head necklace on and I told her she could still keep it for a while if she wanted, then I asked her about the Mr. Frank secret.

GRACE HOLDING
MY NEW ARIZONA
PILLOW

THIS IS NICE!

THE BIG SECRET

Grace asked me to close my bedroom door so no one else could hear and then she said the big secret was that Mr. Frank was an alien. Both of us other Graces screamed, "AN ALIEN?" at the exact same time.

Then the Grace who used to be the Big Meanie started laughing and said no, she was only joking, but that Mr. Frank being an alien would be way more exciting than the real true secret. She said the real true secret was that Mr. Frank was her very own next-door neighbor, and that before he was Mr. Frank the student teacher he used to be called Jeffrey. And that last summer when he was still Jeffrey, he had even baby-sat her and her little sister, Annie, two times. She said that she was really good at calling him Mr. Frank but that he was always forgetting to remember to call her Grace F.

We other two Graces smiled when she said that because it made us feel a whole lot better to know the reason Mr. Frank was always making that mistake. It's harder for old people to change to new ideas. Young people like us can do it much better. Grace told us all about the things she knew about Mr. Frank, and of course we promised not to ever say even one word about any of it to anyone.

THINGS ABOUT MR. FRANK

1 He used to have a girlfriend named Rebecca, but now Grace never sees her anymore.

2 He is really good at playing basketball and almost always makes the basket.

3 He likes to wear T-shirts with the names of rock groups on them when he is not working at our school.

4 He has a dog named Winkie. It is a golden retriever, but Winkie is pretty fat, so he doesn't look so much like  a regular golden retriever.

5 He loves to wear his base-ball cap, which has a picture of a tractor on the front of it.

Grace said Mr. Frank is a nice neighbor, and then both of us other Graces said we thought Mr. Frank was a nice teacher too. I was sure hoping that our project would work out great and he could stay a teacher forever.

All this talking about Mr. Frank being Grace's neighbor made me think about my very own neighbor Mimi, and how I never got to even stand next to her anymore because there was fur stuck on everything

I owned. As soon as the Graces left, I got out the vacuum so I could suck up every single piece of Captain Furry fur in my whole entire room. I had to set the vacuum to the super-suck level, because once a piece of Captain Furry fur is on something it sticks there like it is glued. After cleaning I sat down and drew a new comic because it seemed like forever since I had done one and it is something I really like to do.

MORNING

I asked Mom to make French toast for breakfast because when my empathy power is working super hard this is what I like to eat. Plus, today was going to be the best day ever because I was wearing my Supergirl underwear, Grandma's silver locket, and a shirt and pants with not one single piece of Captain Furry fur anywhere. I know this because I checked it in the mirror two times, two times, which is four, to be extra sure.

FUR-FREE ME

PROJECT DAY

As soon as we got into the classroom, Mr.

Frank said we had to go stand with our group partners. Then one person from each group had to pick a number from a baseball hat. We three Graces all smiled because the hat Mr. Frank was using had the picture of a tractor on the front of it, and that meant it was his favorite hat. I went to pick the number and got number three. This was excellent, because for our project to work right we had to start it in the morning and then not finish it until later in the afternoon.

THE PROJECTS

The first group to do their project was the group of Trevor, Ruth, and Francis. All the boys like Ruth because even though she is a girl, she pretty much likes to do boy things more than girl things. But their project was not just a boy thing. They had a huge pile of mixed-up magnetic letters set up next to a big magnetic tray, a dictionary, and a timer clock.

Francis said that they were going to spell out six words in six minutes and that the audience, which was us, got to pick out the words. Everyone started shouting out words at the same time until Mr. Frank said we all had to calm down and take turns. Once we had told them all the words, Trevor pushed the timer button and they started. Ruth had to look in the dictionary to make sure they'd spelled everything the right way.

It was pretty exciting, and near the end of the time we all started chanting, "Go, go, go," and Mr. Frank and Miss Lois didn't even tell us to stop. They got all the words on the board with only ten seconds left over. It was a great project! I could tell that even Miss Lois thought so because she was smiling.

THEY SPELLED SOME
REALLY GOOD WORDS

The next group to do their project was Mimi, Max, and Sammy. Mr. Frank looked a little surprised when they took off their shoes and socks, but he didn't say anything. Max told the audience, us, that he and Mimi and Sammy were going to make each letter of the alphabet using their bodies and then shout out as many adjectives as they could think of that started with that letter. I couldn't believe how good they were. You could really tell that they had practiced.

THE
AMAZING MIMI

My favorite letter was the N because that was the one where Mimi was upside down doing a handstand, and that was a new trick for her and not at all easy to do.

After the Z and "zany" everyone clapped like crazy and Mimi and Max and Sammy all smiled like crazy. And the whole time I even forgot that I used to think that Sammy was disgusting. While they were putting their socks and shoes back on, Grace, Grace, and I got ourselves organized. We even had a name for our project: it was called What You Lost, which was a pretty excellent name because everybody loses stuff, even rich and famous people.

WHAT YOU LOST

Grace went around the room and gave everyone, even the teachers, a little piece of paper with a number on it. Everyone was going to be part of our project. We told them all to keep their number secret and then the other Grace gave everyone one of the posters she had made. They looked really nice. She made three different kinds so not everyone got the same one.

↑ WE MADE CUTS
SO THAT THE LITTLE
BOTTOM TABS COULD BE
TORN OFF

After that I put all the boxes in a line at the front of the room. Each box had its own beautiful number on the front and a little slit in the top where you could put a note.

EXAMPLE OF SOME OF THE NOTE BOXES

IT WAS NOT SO EASY TO MAKE THESE SLITS ALL PERFECT. THIS ONE IS A LITTLE BIG, BUT IT STILL WORKS.

I could tell that no one had any idea of what we were going to do, which was fine because we were going to explain everything and they were going to love it. I was kind of nervous when I went in front of the class. But when I looked at my two Graces, they made the G sign that Grace who used to be the Big Meanie had just invented that very morning, and seeing that gave me the extra braveness I needed.

HAND G SIGN

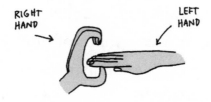

RIGHT HAND → ← LEFT HAND

So I took a big breath and said, "This is called the What I Lost project, and it is about communication . . . the written-down kind. We gave each and every single one of you your very own poster." And then I looked at Miss Lois and Mr. Frank, because we had given them one too. I learned that from Miss Lois. If you want to get someone's attention in a class, you have to give that person the teacher stare. And I wanted Mr. Frank and Miss Lois to notice that we were the only group ever who was including them right in our project with the rest of the class. Then I continued with the explaining part. "On every poster there is a blank space where you have to write down the name of something that you have lost, like a shoe or a button or anything you can think of. You can write about a tangible thing or a not tangible thing." *Tangible* was a big word that Augustine Dupre helped me with, and one that I was sure was going to impress Miss Lois. I told everyone what it meant because *tangible* is not a word that most kids can understand without some explaining to help them. "A *tangible* thing is something that you can hold or feel." And then I wrote some examples on the board so everyone could understand.

TANGIBLE	NOT TANGIBLE
CHAIR	FEELINGS
HAIR	DREAMS
SHIRT	WISHES
CAR	RAINBOWS
APPLE	
HORSE	

I almost wrote down *unicorn* under the not tangible list. It was good I remembered about Sandy, because she would have for sure cried about that again.

Then I filled out my Lost poster right in front of them all so that they would know exactly what to do when it was their turn. "See, right under the word *lost* you write in something you have lost. Like I just did." Lots of kids in my class don't pay attention, so it's a good idea to explain stuff really carefully, as if you are talking to someone in kindergarten or something.

WHAT I WROTE ON MY POSTER

LOST

MY NAME
GRACE!
I REALLY MISS
IT.

When I was finished everyone said "Ooohh" and looked at Miss Lois. She was smiling only a little tiny smile, but still she didn't look mad, so this was a good thing. Then it was time to explain the very end part of the project. I held up my little secret number card so everyone could see it. It had a number 11 on it. I showed them all where to write their secret numbers on their posters. I wrote my number in the square at the top of my poster and on the six little squares on the bottom of the poster.

"Now what?" asked Ruth. Miss Lois made her teacher hand sign that means "If you have a question, please put up your hand." Ruth looked at Miss Lois and then put her hand up. Just like Miss Lois, I pointed at her and said, "Yes?" and she said, "What happens now?"

It was a good question because that was exactly the next thing I was going to talk about. So I said, "Well, when everyone has finished the posters we are going to hang them up all around the class so everyone can walk around the room and read them. When you see a poster that you want to write something about, you pull off one of the little pieces of paper at the bottom and write your message on it. Then you take your message over to the box with the same number on it and drop it inside."

"It's just like the boxes we use on Valentine's Day," shouted Sammy, "except those ones have your name on the front." Mr. Frank said, "Sammy," and Miss Lois gave him her teacher look because he had broken two school rules at the same time, shouting and not putting his hand up. But he was right about the valentines boxes. And it was a good way to explain it to the class. I smiled at him even though he had interrupted me and then gotten in trouble. Mimi could be right — maybe Sammy was kind of okay. Plus, I hadn't seen him pick his nose in ages, which was definitely a good thing.

Sandra Orr put her hand up so I said, "Yes?" and pointed at her. "Can we write more than one message? What if we see two posters we want to write about?" I was glad it was an easy question to answer, and I said, "You can write as many messages as you want."

Then I pointed at Robert Walters because his hand was up too. "Why do we have to keep our posters a secret? What if I want everyone to know it's about me and I wrote it because it's so excellent?" This was a harder question to answer, but I thought about it for a minute and then said, "It's just a rule so no one will get embarrassed." Robert was not my favorite person in the class. He always thought everything he did was wonderful, which it was not. His favorite shirt, which he wore all the time, said I'M NUMBER 1 on the front of it. He was more like number 1,000,000,000,000,000,000, but I don't think all those zeros would fit on it.

And then before anyone could ask any more questions I gave my Graces the secret signal, and all together we said, "Start your posters now!" I was tired and super glad to sit down back at my desk. It's a lot harder to be a teacher than a student. Now I could understand why Mr. Frank was having so many troubles with it.

SO FAR SO GOOD

Mr. Frank let everyone work on the posters until it was time for recess. And the only person who said anything in that whole entire time was Miss Lois. She asked us if it was okay to draw a picture on the poster if we wanted. Of course we three Graces all said okay, because it was an excellent idea. And I was really surprised that such a good idea about drawing was coming from Miss Lois. This whole time I thought she only liked words.

At recess time we stayed to help Mr. Frank put up all the finished posters, and when everyone came back to the class after recess, you could tell that they all thought the posters looked amazing, which they did.

MORE PROJECTS

It was really hard to keep concentrating on the other projects because I was trying to read the posters instead. I just couldn't help it. Mr. Frank must have noticed other people doing it too because he interrupted Gary, Sunni, and Margaret, who were in the middle of their project, and said, "As soon as this next group is finished, everyone will have twenty minutes to walk around the class to look at the Lost posters and put notes in the boxes."

Their project was about changing nouns in the Three Bears story and then reading it to us. It was kind of funny because they changed the bears into princesses and the porridge into silly foods like lollipops,

worm soup, and cupcakes. You could tell
which parts Gary had helped with because
Sunni and Margaret are not the kind of girls
who like disgusting things. After their story
we finally got to go around and read the
posters.

MY FAVORITE POSTERS

I liked this one because I could tell that Miss
Lois made it. No kids drink coffee, plus I

recognized her handwriting. It was proof that she for sure liked our project. At first I was surprised that she likes elephants so much, but then I remembered that she once said she would like to ride on an elephant. It made me wonder if Miss Lois's house was filled with elephant stuff.

**WHAT MIGHT BE IN
MISS LOIS'S HOUSE**

ELEPHANT
FLOWER VASE

ELEPHANT
PLATE

ELEPHANT
TOILET BOWL
SCRUBBER

ELEPHANT
BOWL

FOOT
GOES
IN HERE

ELEPHANT SLIPPER

LOST

MY FAVORITE RED
PEN WITH A LIGHT
UP STAR ON TOP OF IT.

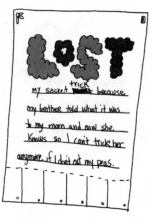

LOST

MY secret ~~trick~~ because
my brother told what it was
to my mom and now she
knows so I can't trick her
anymore if I don't eat my peas.

LOST

MY SHIRT FROM
CANADA WHICH
IS TOO SMALL
SO MOM GAVE IT
AWAY EVEN IF IT WAS MY FAVORITE!

LOST

my plant because
I forgot to give it water
and then it died and it
was too late to save it even
with tons of water.

I wrote notes for five of the posters and then put them in the right numbered box. Mr. Frank was not going to get in trouble this time, I could tell. He was smiling a big smile at Miss Lois, and she was smiling right back at him.

THESE WERE MY NOTES BACK

SORRY ABOUT YOUR CUP.
YOU SHOULD BUY A NEW ONE.
MR. FRANK IS DOING A
REAL GOOD JOB!

OWEN HAS A PEN LIKE
THAT MAYBE HE FOUND
YOURS.

I WOULD LIKE TO KNOW
YOUR SECRET TRICK
BECAUSE I DON'T LIKE PEAS.

I DON'T LIKE WHEN I
GET TOO BIG FOR MY
FAVORITE CLOTHES!

MY MOM ALWAYS KILLS
PLANTS TOO. SHE SAYS
SHE DOESN'T HAVE A
GREEN THUMB MAYBE YOU
DON'T EITHER

WHAT HAPPENED AT LUNCHTIME

I tried to find Mimi so I could tell her that she was the most excellent human *N* I had ever seen, but the Graces found me first and wanted to talk about our project. I was sharing their joy 100 percent, so it was nice to all have lunch together.

MORE AND MORE PROJECTS

There is one thing that I know for sure, and that thing is that I am going to know everything about nouns and other sentence parts and language when these projects are over.

We listened to two more groups and then Mr. Frank gave us another ten minutes to look at the posters one last time. I don't know how I missed it before, but hanging next to the fire alarm was the most saddest Lost poster ever.

It reminded me of how I was feeling when Mimi had her new friend Max following her everywhere so I had to for sure write a note to help this person feel better.

I THOUGHT I LOST MY BEST FRIEND TH TOO BUT I THINK I WAS WRONG BECAUSE IF SOMEONE IS YOUR BEST FRIEND THEN USUALLY, STAY THAT WAY EVEN IF YOU (THEY) THINK NO BECAUSE BEST FRIENDS LOVE EACH OTHER→

AND IT'S REALLY HARD TO JUST TURN OFF LOVE. GOOD LUCK! YOU SHOULD TALK TO HIM/HER.

I had to use both sides of the little paper.

THEN FINALLY WE GOT TO OPEN OUR BOXES

Mr. Frank said we could open our boxes at the end of the day. I was super glad about that, because I was crazy with waiting to see what was inside. I was hoping he wasn't going to make us wait until every single project was finished, because that for sure was going to probably take a week. A week is a long time to be looking at a box and wondering what's inside. That kind of waiting can make you have a hard time with concentrating on anything else, which is the exact kind of thing that makes a teacher angry. I sure hoped Miss Lois was paying attention to how Mr. Frank was making all the right decisions with his teaching.

There were six notes in my box, which means every single little rip-off note got used, and they were all good except for one. If I didn't know the Big Meanie wasn't really a Big Meanie anymore I would have guessed that the bad note was maybe from her, but because I know her now I could tell that it wasn't. So somewhere in the class there was another meanie, but that didn't matter so much because all the other notes were so perfect, especially the one from Mr. Frank, even though he signed his name and didn't keep it a secret. Plus I could tell that the new meanie was only really a mini meanie anyway, and probably just jealous. Still, I kind of wondered who it was.

NOTES THAT WERE IN MY BOX (NUMBER 11)

I LIKE YOUR NAME EVEN THOUGH THERE ARE 4 OF YOU IN THIS CLASS.

Don't worry your Real name will always be the Grace one, not the Just Grace one.

WHAT HAPPENED WHEN THE BELL RANG AT THE END OF THE DAY

Grace came up to me and said that she thought Mr. Frank was for sure going to get a real good mark on this project from Miss Lois. She could tell this because Mr. Frank and Miss Lois were talking and doing lots of smiling. Then Grace gave me a hug and said, "I'll see you later, Grace." "See you, Grace," I said, and I waved a goodbye at her that turned into a hello wave to Mimi, who was watching us.

Mimi walked over real slow, and that was probably because she was scared she was still going to be allergic to me. I couldn't wait to tell her how great she was in the *N,* and how I never could have believed it if I didn't see it with my very own eyes.

Mimi was not as happy as I thought she'd be, and I could tell that because of my empathy power. She said thank you but then didn't want to talk about it anymore. I was hoping she would do a handstand just for me so I could see close up how to do it, but instead she wanted to talk about her poster. "Did you guess which one I did?" asked Mimi.

I looked around the room but I couldn't

decide which one to pick. "That one," said Mimi, and she pointed to the Lost My Best Friend poster next to the fire alarm. I couldn't believe it. Mimi had the saddest poster in the whole class and it was a message all about me.

"Mimi, I'm not lost. I'm right here," I said. "But what about your new Grace friends?" asked Mimi. I could tell that she wasn't believing me 100 percent that she was still my best friend forever. She was feeling the exact same way I used to be feeling about Max and Sammy, except maybe even worse, because I didn't make my poster about it.

MY SECRET HELPER

Sometimes it is really hard to make a person believe something when they think another

thing might really be the truth. Like how
Mimi was thinking that maybe I wanted to
be best friends with the Graces instead of
her, which was 100 percent not the truth.
And if this kind of thing happened, then you
could be wishing that you had a real magic
bead-head necklace to make a wish on so the
not-the-truth feeling would go away.

But I didn't need that because I had
something better,
and as soon as I
showed it to Mimi
she knew that we
were still the best
friends ever. And
when we hugged
she didn't even
have one sneeze!

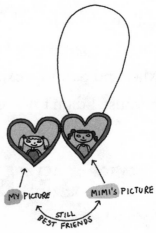

MY PICTURE   MIMI'S PICTURE

STILL
BEST FRIENDS

EPILOGUE

I know about the word *epilogue* because sometimes at the last part of an *Unlikely Heroes* show they put it on the TV screen right before they tell you what the people in the story are doing now. Usually it's not hero stuff, but still, it's kind of fun to know about it. An epilogue is the place where you tell what happened at the end, when the main part of the story is finished. Stuff like how I showed Mimi the note I had written about her Lost poster and how that made her smile a real happy Mimi smile. How Owen gave the red pen he had found back to Sarah, who had lost it. How Mr. Frank was for sure going to get an excellent student-teacher mark because now he and Miss Lois smiled at each other all the time and his face never got red. How standing talking to three other Graces at the same time can be really fun. And then, finally, how playing with four friends can sometimes be just as much fun as playing with just one friend, even when that one friend is your best friend forever.